AF228541

FACT AND FICTION OF THE AMERICAN REVOLUTION

BY TAMMY GAGNE

CONTENT CONSULTANT
Jacqueline Carr, PhD
Associate Professor of Early American History
University of Vermont

Cover image: The Continental army used fifes and drums to communicate orders to large groups of soldiers.

Core Library

An Imprint of Abdo Publishing
abdobooks.com

abdobooks.com

Published by Abdo Publishing, a division of ABDO, PO Box 398166, Minneapolis, Minnesota 55439.

Printed in the United States of America, North Mankato, Minnesota
052021
092021

Cover Photo: Keith Lance/iStockphoto
Interior Photos: Stock Montage/Archive Photos/Getty Images, 4–5; David Cianetti/Shutterstock Images, 8; North Wind Picture Archives/Alamy, 12–13; North Wind Picture Archives, 15, 26–27; ClassicStock/Alamy, 18–19; Niday Picture Library/Alamy, 21, 31, 43, 45; Gerry Embelton/North Wind Picture Archives, 23; Thos D. Murphy/Library of Congress, 34–35; Shutterstock Images, 37; GL Archive/Alamy, 41

Editor: Aubrey Zalewski
Series Designer: Ryan Gale

Library of Congress Control Number: 2020948175

Publisher's Cataloging-in-Publication Data

Names: Gagne, Tammy, author.
Title: Fact and fiction of the American revolution / by Tammy Gagne
Description: Minneapolis, Minnesota : Abdo Publishing, 2022 | Series: Fact and fiction of American history | Includes online resources and index.
Identifiers: ISBN 9781532195105 (lib. bdg.) | ISBN 9781098215415 (ebook)
Subjects: LCSH: United States--History--Revolution, 1775-1783--Juvenile literature. | Political science--History--18th century--Juvenile literature. | Truthfulness and falsehood--Juvenile literature. | Public opinion--Juvenile literature.
Classification: DDC 973.3--dc23

CONTENTS

4

CHAPTER ONE

THE MIDNIGHT RIDE OF PAUL REVERE

Paul Revere mounted his horse just before midnight on April 18, 1775. Revere was a patriot. He opposed British rule. He thought the American colonies should be independent. Revere rode from Boston to Lexington, Massachusetts. He needed to warn fellow patriots John Hancock and Samuel Adams that British soldiers were coming for them. His ride lasted into the early hours of the next morning.

Paul Revere borrowed the horse he rode during his midnight ride from a fellow patriot named John Larkin.

Revere called out to the colonists as his horse galloped. He warned them that British forces from Boston were about to arrive. The soldiers were looking for weapons the colonists were stockpiling. "The British are coming!" Revere is said to have yelled.

"PAUL REVERE'S RIDE"

Henry Wadsworth Longfellow was a New England poet. He told Revere's story in his poem "Paul Revere's Ride." Longfellow wrote it 80 years after the event. Historians say Longfellow was trying to inspire men. He wanted them to join the Union army at the start of the Civil War (1861–1865). But the poem became a source of misinformation for future generations.

Revere is now seen as one of the most important figures of American history. His warning kept the British from gaining the upper hand in the coming war. Revere's ride was a key part in starting the American Revolutionary War (1775–1783). This war won the colonists their independence from Great Britain. It also led to the creation of the United States. But the story about Revere is one of many tales from the time that include as much fiction as fact.

In 1775, the American colonists saw themselves as British. So Revere would not have called the soldiers British. He likely warned that the "regulars" were coming. This was what the colonists called the British soldiers. Colonists nicknamed them this because the British soldiers were in the regular British Army. Revere also did not make his famous journey alone. William Dawes and Samuel Prescott also helped. These men were just a few of the many people who spread the important message.

It is true that Revere played a key role in this major event. In addition to his ride, he thought of a secret way to warn minutemen. These were volunteers who fought for the colonies. They were ready to fight at a minute's notice. But even minutemen needed warning time to defend themselves. Revere told them to watch

the steeple of Christ Church in Boston. It is now known as the Old North Church. If the regulars were coming by land, a single lantern would be lit there. Two lanterns would mean the enemy was coming across the Charles River. Knowing this would help the minutemen prepare.

The lanterns were Revere's idea. But he could not make it happen alone. Robert John Newman and

A LESSER-KNOWN RIDE

Revere's was not the only important horseback ride of the Revolution. In 1777, 16-year-old Sybil Ludington made a ride of her own. She rode approximately 40 miles (64 km). She tried to warn colonists in New York of an attack in Connecticut. Ludington's ride was not as successful as Revere's. She was not able to spread the word to the colonists in time. But many historians think she was still an important part of that historic night. Her bravery and action made her stand out as a patriot of the American Revolution.

A statue of Paul Revere stands near the Old North Church in Boston, Massachusetts.

Captain John Pulling placed the lanterns in the church. Revere was just one of many heroes that day. Still, he ended up with all the credit. The others are often left out of the story completely.

WHY ARE FALSE STORIES SO POPULAR?

Stories from history often get reduced to a few details. These simple facts are easy to teach and remember. The more a story is told, the more people assume it is true. Myths can become valued parts of a nation's history. And the American Revolution was so important that its stories have shaped how people think of the United States today.

Many people are drawn to the most exciting versions of a tale. But many of these stories are inaccurate. Some popular stories contain a mixture of truth and falsehoods. Others are complete fiction. Researching is the best way to know the truth behind each story.

STRAIGHT TO THE
SOURCE

Paul Revere and William Dawes carried written messages with news of the British troops. The two men split up. Historian David Hackett Fischer shared details of the events on April 18, 1775:

The messengers took different routes. William Dawes left town across Boston Neck—no small feat. He had to pass a narrow gate, closely guarded by British sentries who stopped all suspicious travelers. . . .

Paul Revere made ready to leave in a different direction, by boat to Charlestown. His journey was not a solitary act. Many people in Boston helped him on his way—so many that Paul Revere's ride was truly a collective effort. He would be very much surprised by his modern image as the lone rider of the Revolution.

Source: David Fischer. *Paul Revere's Ride*. Oxford University Press, 1994. pp. 97–98.

CONSIDER YOUR AUDIENCE

Adapt this passage for a different audience, such as your younger friends. Write a blog post conveying this same information for the new audience. How does your post differ from the original text and why?

STAMP ACT
THE FOLLY OF ENGLAND
THE RUIN OF AMERICA

TOO MANY TAXES?

Many accounts of the American Revolution blame unfair taxation for causing the war. In the mid-1700s, the British government began passing new tax laws. These included the Stamp Act in 1765 and the Townshend Acts in 1767. The Stamp Act placed a tax on all documents printed in the colonies. The Townshend Acts added taxes to many popular items, including glass and paper. Colonists now had to pay more money to Great Britain for goods. The British government even taxed tea.

In 1765, colonists protested the Stamp Act.

As the story usually goes, many colonists were outraged by all these taxes. Some people protested the fees. By 1770, most of the Townshend Acts were repealed. But the tax on tea remained. Some colonists who opposed the tax on tea banded together. On December 16, 1773, more than 100 colonists sneaked onto British ships in Boston Harbor. They dumped more than 300 chests of tea into the ocean. This protest is now called the Boston Tea Party. There were many related protests. These rebellions raised tensions between the

THE QUARTERING ACT

The Quartering Act was another controversial law that Britain passed. It stated that colonists must provide food and lodging to British soldiers. Many films about the American Revolution show British soldiers barging into homes. This law did give soldiers permission to eat and sleep on colonists' property. But the soldiers did not typically take over people's private homes. Instead, they mostly stayed in taverns, inns, and stables.

Members of a group called the Sons of Liberty were among the protesters who boarded the ships during the Boston Tea Party.

colonists and Britain. Eventually the colonists decided to fight for their independence.

THE REAL ISSUE

Taxation was indeed a key issue that led to the American Revolution. But many stories get some facts wrong. The colonists did not like taxes. But the amounts were not outrageous for the era. The average person living in Great Britain at the time paid approximately 26 shillings each year in taxes. The average colonist paid just 1 shilling per year.

Some historians note that the average colonist wasn't affected by the taxes. The merchants paid the new fees. They passed the fees to their customers. But these customers mostly lived in cities. Many people lived in rural areas. They did not buy as much from the merchants. They either used what they already owned or made the items they needed. Colonists in the cities were often wealthier. These colonists did not welcome taxes. But the taxes were not a burden to them.

The taxes themselves weren't the main thing angering the colonists. Colonists were much more upset that they did not have a say in the new tax laws. British citizens had rights called English liberties. One was the right to elect officials to represent them in government. The representatives would make decisions about taxes and other important matters. However, the colonists were not represented by those who were taxing them. This angered them. They felt that Great Britain was taking away their liberties. A common protest was "No taxation without representation!"

EXPLORE ONLINE

Chapter Two discusses why colonists resisted the taxes that Great Britain made them pay. The website below goes into more depth on the Stamp Act. How is the information from the website the same as the information in Chapter Two? What new information did you learn from the website?

THE STAMP ACT

abdocorelibrary.com/fact-fiction-american-revolution

AMERICAN REVOLUTIONARIES

The American Revolution did not happen without warning. As the stories go, the relationship between the colonies and Great Britain worsened over time. Patriots wanted to fight for their freedom. They prepared for war. Part of this preparation involved gathering weapons and ammunition.

The British army suspected that the colonists were gathering supplies. On the morning of April 19, 1775, approximately 700 British soldiers received orders. They were to travel to Concord, Massachusetts. A large stash of weapons was hidden there. The colonial

Approximately 80 militiamen were waiting when the British soldiers arrived at Lexington.

PATRIOT'S DAY

In 1894, Lexington asked the state of Massachusetts to name April 19 Lexington Day. The city wanted to mark the occasion of the famous shot heard around the world. But Concord said the shot had actually happened in its own borders. Concord wanted the day named for its city instead. Governor Frederic T. Greenhalge refused to take sides. He did not choose either option. He named the third Monday of April Patriot's Day. The holiday is still celebrated each year in Massachusetts, Connecticut, and Maine.

militia could not fight without their weapons.

As the British soldiers approached, the colonial militia realized it was outnumbered. The militia had approximately 500 men, mostly farmers. But these patriots stood up to the British. One of the patriots fired upon the red-coated soldiers. In 1837, poet Ralph Waldo Emerson wrote the poem "Concord Hymn" about the event. In it he called the militiaman's action "the shot heard

Approximately 400 militiamen at the North Bridge forced the British soldiers to retreat.

round the world." Emerson's words suggested this shot started the Revolution.

THE TRUE BEGINNING

This popular tale is not completely true. The British soldiers did travel to Concord in search of weapons. But the British soldiers first met the militia in Lexington, Massachusetts. This is where the first shot was fired. No one knows which side fired first. After the first shot, the British began shooting. The patriots retreated. The first real battle happened a few hours later at the North Bridge in Concord. In June, colonist leaders formed the official Continental army to oppose the British.

NOT ALL WERE FIGHTERS

Among the biggest American Revolution myths is the idea that all colonists wanted to fight. Relations between Great Britain and the colonies had worsened. But there were periods of quiet. Most colonists opposed Great Britain's actions. But many did not want war. They saw those in Great Britain as fellow British citizens.

Additionally, feelings about the British depended on where people lived. Areas that were doing well were slow to support the war. Many merchants in big cities such as New York and Philadelphia did not want to cause trouble with Great Britain. They liked things the way they were.

The colonists who sided with the British government were called loyalists. They paid a high price. The colonial governments that supported the

A CONTINENTAL SOLDIER

The typical Continental soldier had to carry essential items. Some of these items are shown below. The bayonet was a blade that could fit at the end of the musket. The knapsack held a blanket, clothes, and other necessary items. The haversack was a cloth bag that held food. And the canteen held water. What does the image below show about what it was like to be a Continental soldier?

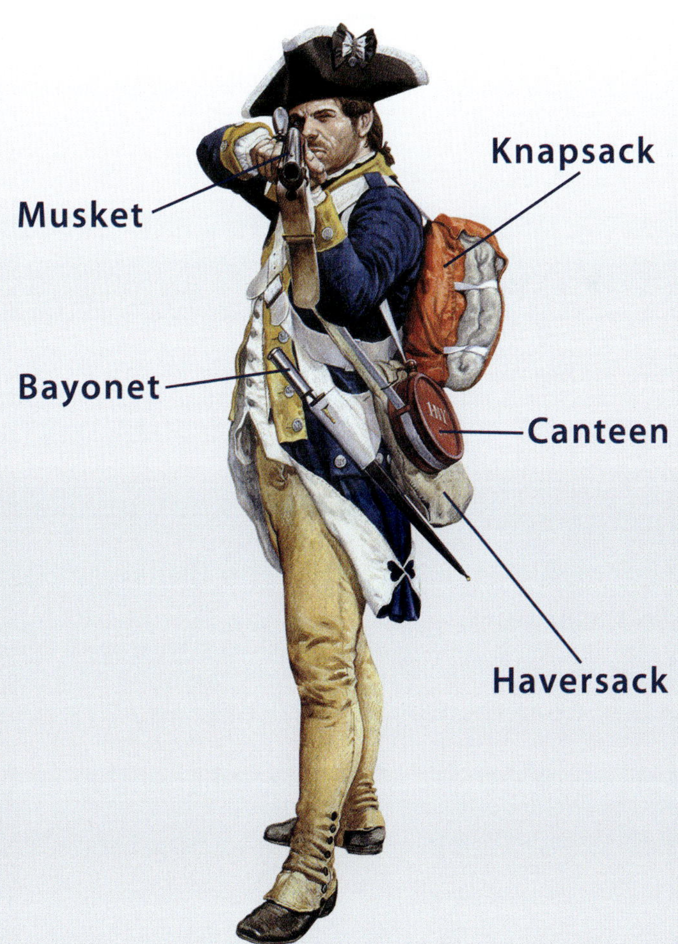

war seized their property. They then sold it to help pay for the war. Loyalists were treated poorly in society. The patriots called them traitors.

NOT JUST FARMERS

Many stories describe the Continental army as disorganized groups of simple farmers. They also show the soldiers as having little experience in warfare. The Continental army was not unskilled. The British soldiers had more experience. But many Continental soldiers had served in a previous war.

The colonists were strong opponents in the Revolution. First, they had valuable experience in warfare. They had learned the basics, including how to handle weapons. Second, they were familiar with the land. They used their knowledge of the area to their advantage during battles. They knew many of the best spots for hiding, watching, and attacking. Still, they were not a superior army. In the early years of the war, there was a lot of chaos among the Continental army. And many deserted. But their skills and experience grew over the course of the war.

HOW THE PATRIOTS WON THE WAR

Winning a war is complicated. Even the best armies and strategies do not guarantee a victory. Stories from the American Revolution often make the patriots seem like sure winners. But the Continental army was not the likely victor. The Revolution was a long and difficult war that could have gone differently.

FIGHTING STRATEGY

Many stories claim that the patriots' use of rifles gave them the upper hand. These tales usually describe Continental soldiers attacking

British soldiers fought in tight line formations.

from a distance. This position gave the patriots a clear advantage. The British soldiers were used to facing

their enemies on battlefields. They did not suspect that shots would come from so far away.

But there is a flaw in these stories. Most soldiers on both sides used muskets, not rifles. Muskets were easy to load. They were also accurate. But the target had to be fewer than 100 yards (91 m) away. This required the armies to get close to each other. Rifles could hit their targets

A GREAT LEADER BUT NOT A STRATEGIST

George Washington was a general in the American Revolution. Later he became the first US president. Some stories describe him as a brilliant war strategist. But they exaggerate these skills. Historians say Washington took too long to make important decisions. This led to several early losses in the war. He also tried to defend areas that were too large for his army. Washington admitted that strategy was not among his strengths. But his ability to see his own shortcomings and use all his resources were part of what made him such a great leader.

from at least twice that distance. But they were much more difficult to load. This could cost a soldier valuable time in battle. Some patriots did use rifles. But they were not used enough to be a deciding factor.

Fighting in the South was different from fighting in the North. The South had many loyalists. Sometimes there was even fighting between the patriots and the loyalists. The British assumed that the loyalists would help them win the war. But there were not as many loyalists as the British thought. And many people who had not taken sides became patriots. The patriots in the South often relied on guerrilla tactics. They could hide among the locals. If the British had better understood the colonies in the South, the war might have had a different outcome.

BATTLE OF SARATOGA

For several years it seemed likely that Great Britain would win the war. After all, the British soldiers had more training and resources. They also won many of the early battles. But the British made a mistake. British general William Howe was supposed to help General John Burgoyne in New York. But Howe did not, and he instead captured Philadelphia, Pennsylvania. Without Howe's support, General Burgoyne had to surrender to American forces after the Battle of Saratoga in 1777. This New York battle is often called the turning point of the American Revolution. A turning point is an event that changes an outcome.

British general John Burgoyne, *second from the left*, surrendered to American general Horatio Gates, *center*.

Many facts support that this was the war's turning point. In the five months before the battle, the Continental soldiers killed, wounded, or captured more than 1,300 British soldiers. The American victory outside Saratoga, New York, worsened Great Britain's position even further. By the time the battle was finished, an additional 5,895 British troops had surrendered.

The British army had lost nearly one-quarter of its soldiers in the colonies.

The outcome at Saratoga was significant. The victory convinced France to side with the Americans. France had not wanted to align with the colonists until it seemed likely that they could win. But Saratoga was not the single turning point. Several other battles played deciding roles in the war. They included victories in Massachusetts, New Jersey, and South Carolina. It is exciting to pinpoint one key turning point. But the truth is that most war victories are the results of many events. The American Revolution ended in 1781. After its loss at the Battle of Yorktown in Virginia, Great Britain decided to stop fighting the American colonies over their independence.

STRAIGHT TO THE
SOURCE

Historian David McCullough shared his views on the most significant event of the American Revolution. It was the retreat after the Battle of Brooklyn in 1776. As he saw it, even the weather played a role:

For me the key event is the Continental Army's escape from Brooklyn after being soundly defeated in the first full-scale battle of the war. . . . On the one hand, Washington's role in the escape was [leadership] at its best. On the other hand, circumstances beyond his or anyone's control played a part almost beyond belief. If the wind had been blowing in a different direction, the British would have been able to bring their warships up the East River and seal off any possibility of escape for Washington and his troops. The war and the chances of an independent United States of America could have ended there and then.

Source: "Interview with David McCullough." *History News Network*, June 2005, hnn.us. Accessed 19 June 2020.

WHAT'S THE BIG IDEA?

Take a close look at this passage. What connections does McCullough make between the weather and Washington's escape from Brooklyn? What are two pieces of evidence that McCullough uses to support his point?

SYMBOLS OF INDEPENDENCE

One of the best-known stories from the American Revolution is about Betsy Ross. A famous painting called *The Birth of Old Glory* shows her with the first official American flag. Artist Edward Percy Moran created the painting. It shows Ross presenting the flag she had made to George Washington. Thirteen red and white stripes wave across the fabric banner. In the upper left corner, 13 white stars form a circle over a blue background. The number of stars and stripes represent the 13 colonies that became the first US states after the war.

Edward Percy Moran painted *The Birth of Old Glory* around 1917.

Both the painting and the flag are powerful images of independence. They also help tell one of the few stories about a woman in the American Revolution.

Betsy Ross is credited with making an important symbol of freedom for the new nation. However, the story about her involvement may be more fiction than fact.

The tale about Ross was passed down by family members to her grandson William Canby. The story was not well known until he shared it with the Historical Society of Pennsylvania in 1870.

THE AMERICAN FLAGS

Early American flags looked very different from the flag Americans know today. The most recent version came in 1960. It added the fiftieth star when Hawaii became a state. Why do you think leaders thought it was important to change the flag as the country grew?

It likely served as the inspiration for Moran's painting. Historians have tried to find proof of the story. But so far no record of the tale before Canby's version has been found. No one has proven the story false. But no one has been able to confirm it either.

THE FOURTH OF JULY

Independence Day in the United States is a big event. People throughout the nation celebrate the country's birthday each year on the Fourth of July. They plan picnics, attend parades, and watch fireworks displays. Many believe this holiday marks the signing of the Declaration of Independence. This document is one of the most important documents in the nation's history. Fifty-six men signed the document. It told Great Britain that the American colonies were no longer under British rule. It also announced the country's new name, the United States of America. Almost everything about this holiday is based in fact. The only thing wrong is the date.

The Declaration of Independence was actually signed long after July 4. Thomas Jefferson and four other men had taken on the task of writing the document. On June 28, 1776, they presented it to the Second Continental Congress. This group governed the colonies as they made their way through the war and the early days of the new nation. It included representatives from all 13 colonies. Many of them suggested changes to the document. On July 2, they declared

SOMETHING TO CELEBRATE

John Adams signed the Declaration of Independence. He was sure future Americans would celebrate July 2. In 1776 he said, "[Independence Day] will be the most memorable [event], in the History of America. I am apt to believe that it will be celebrated, by succeeding Generations, as the great anniversary Festival. . . . It ought to be solemnized with Pomp and Parade with [shows], Games, Sports, Guns, Bells, Bonfires and Illuminations from one End of this continent to the other from this Time forward forever more."

independence from Great Britain. And two days later, they approved the final document. This is why July 4 appears at the top of the declaration. Most of the representatives added their signatures to the document on August 2. A few signed it even later.

It is unlikely that the date of the Independence Day holiday will change. The Fourth of July is now cemented into the hearts of the people as the nation's birthday. But knowing the whole story is important. People must separate fact from fiction to truly learn about history.

Thomas Jefferson, *in red*, and his committee present their draft of the Declaration of Independence to John Hancock, *seated*.

IMPORTANT DATES

1765

Great Britain passes the Stamp Act. It introduces a tax on all documents printed in the American colonies.

1767

Great Britain passes the Townshend Acts. These laws introduce taxes to the American colonies. The taxes are on commonly purchased items such as glass and paper.

1773

On December 16, colonists dump more than 300 chests of tea into Boston Harbor during the Boston Tea Party.

1775

On April 18 and 19, Paul Revere and others make their famous rides to warn their fellow patriots that regular British soldiers are coming.

1775

The American Revolution begins with the Battles of Lexington and Concord on April 19.

1776
On July 4, the Second Continental Congress approves the Declaration of Independence. Representatives from most of the colonies sign the Declaration of Independence on August 2.

1777
The Battle of Saratoga takes place in New York. It is one of several events that lead to the colonists' victory in the American Revolution.

1870
Betsy Ross's grandson William Canby submits a story about her making the first official American flag to the Historical Society of Pennsylvania.

STOP AND THINK

Surprise Me

Chapter Three discusses some of the key events from the American Revolution. After reading this book, what two or three facts about the war did you find most surprising? Write a few sentences about each fact. Why did you find each fact surprising?

Say What?

Studying the American Revolution can mean learning a lot of new vocabulary. Find five words in this book you've never seen before. Use a dictionary to find out what they mean. Then write the meanings in your own words and use each word in a new sentence.

Dig Deeper

After reading this book, what questions do you still have about the American Revolution? With an adult's help, find a few reliable sources that can help answer your questions. Write a paragraph about what you learned.

Take a Stand

Some misinformation about the American Revolution comes from artwork and famous poems, such as "Paul Revere's Ride" and "Concord Hymn." Why do you think artistic works sometimes change the facts? Do you think it is okay for artistic works to not perfectly follow the truth? Why or why not?

GLOSSARY

ammunition
a supply of bullets or shells for firearms

desert
to leave military service without permission

guerrilla tactics
irregular warfare in which a small group uses surprise attacks and property damage against a larger force

merchant
a person who trades goods

militia
a group of citizens who serve as a military force during emergencies

minutemen
militia members who could be ready to fight at a moment's notice

musket
a long-barreled gun fired from the shoulder

regiment
a unit of troops in an army

repeal
to take away or end by authority

shilling
a British monetary unit used in the colonial era

stockpiling
building a supply of something

ONLINE RESOURCES

To learn more about facts and fiction of the American Revolution, visit our free resource websites below.

Visit **abdocorelibrary.com** or scan this QR code for free Common Core resources for teachers and students, including vetted activities, multimedia, and booklinks, for deeper subject comprehension.

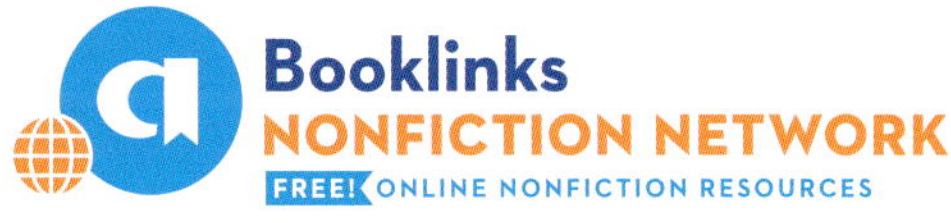

Visit **abdobooklinks.com** or scan this QR code for free additional online weblinks for further learning. These links are routinely monitored and updated to provide the most current information available.

LEARN MORE

Harris, Duchess. *Boston Tea Party*. Abdo Publishing, 2018.

Krull, Kathleen. *A Kids' Guide to the American Revolution*. Harper, 2018.

INDEX

About the Author

Tammy Gagne has written dozens of books for both adults and children. Her recent titles include *Fact and Fiction of American Colonization* and *Fact and Fiction of American Invention*. She lives in northern New England with her husband, her son, and a menagerie of pets.